MOUNTAIN LAUREL
LETHAL

MOUNTAIN LAUREL
LETHAL

A Docksteder Tale

PAUL BUCHANAN

BUCHANAN BOOKS

BUCHANAN BOOKS

PO Box 535

Tryon, NC 28782

info@BuchananBooks.com

ISBN-13: 978-0-9995430-4-7 (paperback)

ISBN-13: 978-0-9995430-5-4 (ebook)

Library of Congress Control Number:
2019936273

Buchanan Books, Tryon, NC

For sex and violence, it's a pretty good story—if you're into that sort of thing.

—Barron Docksteder

Top of the Bluff
Tryon, NC

Docksteder's three requisites for an otherwise struggling writer to become an author (success optional) may have omitted a couple of things. The first, and the only one I'm relatively certain of, is atmosphere. I was all set to start work on a new book when we got at least a foot of snow and lost our cable so no internet for research and no TV. Thank God for the backup generator and a full tank of propane. And even with adequate central heating, a snowy winter demands the use of a fireplace if you have one, and we do.

The three of us cuddling there, watching the snow through the skylight, was more than nice and certainly removed any frustration I had over the loss of the internet. And then when I took Great Beast out into the portico for a bio-break and looked down the bluff-trail with all its memories, the original story idea didn't seem so damned hot either. If I was not to waste a lot of time waiting for spring, I needed some inspiration, and fortunately, I had it—Dock-steder's library.

I'd mostly been through the big three-ring binders and the steno pads, but there were some boxes of things he was working on in drawers under the bookshelves. Each box held a single manuscript, unfinished and certainly unpolished. Barron was a firm believer in stuffing the first draft of something he liked in a drawer for at least six, maybe eight, weeks. That way, when he brought it out for the next round, he'd see it with a clear mind and a fresh pair of eyes.

I pulled out this piece I think he was working on just before he died. Perhaps the reason it caught me was that it seemed at least semi-autobiographical.

I looked out the window and watched the snow feather its way down for a minute. What the hell. What else was I going to do?

I modernized a few bits, tightened up some areas, and finished the damn thing.

Whether the events and people in the story are real or not, I can't say. Nor can I say with certainty whether Barron intended himself as the central figure. But you gotta admit: It sure does sound like him.

MOUNTAIN LAUREL LETHAL

By

B. R. Docksteder

CHAPTER 1

I've lost track of time here, so bear with me.

I remember Charlottesville and being in that fascinating dome that Thomas Jefferson designed to start the university. There was a knock-down, drag-out with some of the English department on writing. I was doing the knocking-down, so they were dragging me out. They invited me and paid me. What did they expect? I remember I wanted to go to Monticello, but I had to get to Asheville, and I wasn't sure... Damn. Anyway, next morning, I tanked up on fuel and food and headed west. Caught the Blue Ridge Parkway south for a quick stop at Overlook No. 13. I had found out a few years ago that Terry Brooks lied. I waited half an hour and never saw a dragon, a beautiful witch, or anything like a magic kingdom. Can't imagine a good writer doing anything that mean to us poor romantics, so I stopped again to look around and maybe see where the inspiration came from. Then it rained.

My neat all-wheel-drive Audi coupe has good wipers and tires. I may slow down, but I don't usually stop for rain. Except this big damn lightning and thunder storm stopped me. I was beginning to think that Brooks was getting even with me for doubting him. I sat for the better part of an hour wondering why I hadn't checked the CDs that had started life in the console almost two years ago. Finally, it eased up enough for me to see across the road, so I decided to give it a try. They keep the Parkway in pretty good shape, but it is not straight. Twenty, maybe occasionally thirty, MPH was it for almost another hour. And then I was lost.

Somehow I'd passed the exit that would have taken me to Roanoke. The good-sized town probably had a decent hotel. But it was too late to get there tonight. Plenty of time to hit Asheville tomorrow, right? Finally, I found a place to pull off and concentrate my eyeballs on the AAA TripTik that was too fucking small. Damn road atlas slipped under the seat. Crap. I had no idea where I was going. Figured

I may as well keep on. Then a piece of luck. Rain stopped, and there was still a smidge of daylight left. About five miles farther down this no-numbered road, and I came to a three-way intersection. Just off the road to my right, I saw a couple of big stone posts on either side of a neatly tended driveway running uphill a hundred yards or so to an impressive looking old three- or four-story house. Probably antebellum, if you're into that kind of thing. Fifteen minutes later, and I could have missed the sign.

Mountain Laurel Lodge
Bed and Breakfast

Lost, tired, damp but not defeated… Why not. The first half of the driveway was asphalt, very smooth and two cars wide if you were careful. Halfway up the hill, it turned to gravel. Smooth and safe but definitely noisy. All the way up from the road, the drive was lined by these big well-trimmed bushes. It became a circle as I reached the front of the building, but there was obviously an extension that went around the place. Eight or ten steps led up to the porch that protected the double doors of the entrance and about half of the front of the building. Some rocking chairs and two low tables gave it a staged homey look. Before I got to the top step, light from a fixture suspended in the middle of the porch ceiling indicated some likely habitation. And it was female.

"Hi. I'm Laurel, and you're welcome. But I don't see that we have a reservation for you, Mister…"

"No… No, you wouldn't have—unless you're awfully good with tea leaves."

She laughed. "Tarot cards actually. But come on in. Speaking of tea, would you care for some?"

"Coffee if you have it made. Is it possible to get a room for the night?"

"Coffee just dripped through in the kitchen. And if you're willing to pay Bellagio penthouse prices, I'm sure we can find you a room—maybe even with a bath."

She turned and walked away, leaving a slight scent of Dior behind her and a vision of some well-shaped calves over three-inch heels.

I would say that for a guy traveling, with no commitment to wife or the like, it may have seemed better than just a dry sleeping bag on a hunting trip. Laurel was attractive, coiffed, well-dressed, and an interesting bit of a smart-ass. I heard a phone ring, heard her talking for a while, then some music—New York café music. A few minutes later, she walked back in with a tray. Along with the coffee, there were some cookies. Macaroons, I think.

"Third cancellation due to that frigging storm!" she said. She didn't seem at all inclined to apologize for the f-word. "Have you eaten?"

"Only a cookie—very recently."

"Tell you what, cook's gone, but she had some things ready to fix for the people with reservations who should have gotten here earlier. I'm sure I can fix us something if you want to come out and help."

"Or maybe I can do the cooking, and you can help." I started to take off my jacket.

"Wow, this may be my lucky day! But hold on a sec. You want to get your luggage or something? You can leave your car where it is tonight."

Laurel led me up the stairs and just a short distance down the hall. I thought it was a little strange, but the numbers 525 were in shiny brass on the door. I almost expected an electronic card-lock, but she used a rather heavy door key then handed it to me. Then the weird started.

I'm fairly sure that most people seeing that old-style but solid building would have expected an antique ambience as part of the usual bed-and-breakfast happening.

What we had here was a round, at least queen-sized bed with a thick—and probably soft—mattress, mirrors on three walls, and a bath with Jacuzzi. I hung up my leather suit bag in the ample closet, dropped my hold-everything backpack, and expected to see Laurel waiting in the door. She was several steps down the hall.

"We'll take the back steps. Short-cut to the kitchen," she said.

I rolled up my sleeves and walked toward her. "Lay on, McLaurel. You're trying to get me lost."

"I think that's Macduff," she said. "And anyway, never on the first night." And she laughed.

Okay... A well-read smart-ass. The kitchen was neat enough, reasonably well set up for commercial work. I found salmon, lots of veggies, but the medaillon of beef and some broccoli appealed. Cook had made some sauce for the beef. I did a little mayonnaise, cheese, and lemon for the broccoli. Laurel set a table in the kitchen while I heated and properly stirred everything. Turned out pretty damn well, even if I do say so. Laurel found some good Médoc. And there I was. Still about three hundred miles from where I should have been but having good food, good wine, and a lovely but kind of different dinner companion. And here she was again, now wearing a flouncy hostess-style apron over the attractive upper-level-management-style dress. And then, of course, there was the bedroom—and the music. Had I stumbled into a corner of that kingdom I'd been looking for up the Parkway?

We ate, we drank, we talked... I don't remember about what. Laurel got up and made coffee in one of those hotel-style quick-drip-for-two coffee makers. They work well if you use the right coffee—and she did. While standing there waiting for it, she eased out of the neat high-heeled shoes.

"Sorry about that," she said. "Been a long day."

"Shucks. And I was just getting ready to ask you to dance."

"Don't believe a word of it. You can probably dance, but I'll bet it's the last thing on your mind when you're with a woman."

"And what were we betting?" I asked. "Never mind. You won."

She laughed.

"So tell me about the modern rooms in this ancient building."

"Oh… Complicated," she said. "First of all, it's not an ancient building. Barely five years old. Just built to look… Whatever it is. I'm sure there never was any really antique furniture in the place. I got the building and a few acres—I thought—on a bankruptcy sale. The losers had managed to strip about all the good stuff in the place. Trying to re-do the building in antiques would have cost a fortune—times two! So… I called a couple of people I knew who were in the hotel business, and they gave me some names. Two of them bid against each other and…that's the story." She sipped the coffee. "One of them had just finished a remodel on a big hotel in Reno. He was careful about what he removed. Pretty nice where you are, nice enough on the second and third levels. Since you did the cooking, I'm giving you a discount. Plus 2 percent." At least she smiled.

"Help any if I do the dishes?"

"Have to question your intelligence," she said. "Probably make it more." She didn't smile. "You want a call in the morning? How 'bout 7:30?"

"Not too early for you?"

"Yes… But I've got a computer call system. And your door won't unlock until after eight o'clock. Come on. Show you a secret."

Laurel took a final sip of coffee, bent to pick up her pumps, and stood. She held out a hand and led me back into the hall. A little further toward the rear of the building, we reached an elevator door. She led me back toward 525 and waited for me to unlock it.

So then I was really wondering what was expected here. I opened the door, and Laurel had not moved away. I turned back toward her and slowly raised my right hand, thinking a gentle shoulder hug might be in order. But she took my right hand in her own in a grip that could have signaled we were going to arm wrestle.

"Your kitchen skills are impressive. I'm sure that isn't what you do, but still… And I enjoyed the company. Breakfast is a kitchen buffet—whenever you get there. Goodnight."

And in her stocking feet, Laurel headed for the broad front stairway.

The tub and bubbles didn't interest me, but the shower was great. Looking up to check my watch before I switched off the light, I noticed that the circular molding on the ceiling followed the curve of the bed. I wasn't doing too well on bets tonight, but this had to have been a frame for a mirror. Maybe the Reno remodelers hadn't been careful enough. Somehow, I didn't think I'd ask.

It was just after 7:15 when something in my brain, and not the computer-call system, popped me awake. I was packing my stuff in the leather suit bag when I got the call. No need to hurry. No one on the line. When I was getting off the elevator, I did hear a voice, a male voice. In the kitchen, it was a little louder, seeming to come from the dining room. Cook was quite an attractive woman with a really good tan, not quite middle-aged. She told me politely to help myself, pointing to the buffet setup, and left through an outside door. I found a tray. The scrambled eggs looked good. Couple of strips, toast, juice, and coffee. I backed through the door into the dining room and the talking stopped—but not for long.

"Why don't you go on back in the kitchen, buddy," the man said. "This lady and I got some business."

"No we don't, Jerome," Laurel said a bit loudly. "He's a guest, and he's..."

"Guest my ass! Single guy with a Virginia plate!"

He pulled a gun, and he brought it out fast. Definitely not his first draw. It looked like a Glock, shorter model. Could have been a 9mm but I'd have bet on a .380 cal. But then…From his left hand, a pair of handcuffs hit the table.

"Get 'em on, Laurel, or Lana, or whatever you're calling yourself now. I've already called him. Private jet at Charlotte when we get there. Now…"

"Wait a minute," I said stupidly. "If you're a cop…" Then I saw it, heard it, and felt something in my right upper chest that I didn't like. The son of a bitch shot me!

I've been around a lot of guns—short, long, all kinds—but I've never been standing just two feet away from the open muzzle of one when it was fired. I dropped the food tray toward the table. The bullet didn't knock me ass-over-appetite like they do in the movies, but I felt like I was leaning backward. I thought I was trying to get my balance, but nothing seemed to be working right. To make it worse, I felt lightheaded, and my vision faded into a gray-out mode. Yep, I was falling. Then I heard it again. I didn't feel anything, but why was the son of a bitch trying to kill me twice?

CHAPTER 2

For those of you who have had the pleasure of awakening from major surgery and a general anesthetic, I'll skip the fun details. One thing though, it ain't fun. The only good thing I remember was the sudden realization that I was actually alive. Still foggy here, but I think it was on the second day that my head cleared enough to try to get some sense out of the surgeon about what had happened. He came into the room about eight o'clock on what I think was the third day with a small group and said he'd be back around noon and we could talk. He was as good as his word—came back with his lunch. I'd have traded him everything but my Rolex for one of his sandwiches.

"Did you know the person who shot you?" Dr. Finnigan asked.

"Never saw him before. Heard..." And suddenly my brain sort of began to work. "Heard someone call him Jerome. I just asked him if he was a cop and *boom*, that was it."

Dr. Finnigan pulled a small clear bottle from his coat pocket. It rattled a little. I struggled for a second to focus on it. It looked like a beat-on pistol slug. "This a present for my experience?" I asked.

"'Fraid not. FBI put a hold on it. Our pathologist has been keeping up with some of the forensic lit. The hole in the end of the slug is homemade he said, and undercut. He took a sample and ran it in the mass spectrometer of the clinical lab. Not the best for critical toxicology, but he got part of an answer. They got a hit on fentanyl and a bit of some organic thing they weren't sure of. When the fed's get it, I guess we'll know. But something else they'll want to know is why were you the target?"

"Doc, if I knew that I wouldn't have been there— not even close. But, hey… What about the other one? The other slug."

"There is no other one, friend. Only found one hole in you. If they fired twice, they must have missed. The metal buckle on the top of your leather jacket pocket helped you some—at least on penetration. Slowed it down but pushed it up a tad. Caught a branch of the subclavian artery and let you bleed a little more. Whoever was putting pressure on it and giving you CPR did a good job."

"Damn. I was totally out of it."

Dr. Finnigan started to leave but there was one more thing I had to find out.

"You get much of this around here—gunshots?" I asked.

"Enough to remember how. But not as much as I did in my residency down in Charlotte. Whenever we were on night-call, if we didn't have at least one GSW, the whole city was asleep." He laughed tiredly. "Make sure we have an address and phone number, and we'll let you know what was in this mess."

"Oh, Doc… One other thing. Are these doped-up slugs peculiar to around here?"

"No… Oh, no. You're my first. Hennison, the pathologist, checked it out. Mostly out west. Nevada and California. Around Las Vegas, I guess they use them so they can still collect the gambling debts." He shrugged and turned toward the door. "California… No idea. Gangs, maybe."

It was almost two weeks before Finnigan and company agreed to let me go. Had to wait until my lung expanded, hemoglobin went up, all that jazz. Anyway, I sounded totally stupid, which I was, during the exit interview with the police. One of the officers offered to drive me back down to the lodge since my car was still parked in the circle there and the owner of the business seemed to have disappeared.

Now are you beginning to feel the weird? Wait, there's more.

While on the way, I checked to make sure I had my room key. Then it just seemed right to check my wallet. My driver's license was still there along with everything else—except one of my two credit cards. Probably a little late to cancel it now. And then after I'd checked to see if my car would start and made sure the room key would open the main door of the lodge, I said goodbye to the cop a little too quickly. My key to 525 let me into a room with a guy handcuffed, gagged, and bleeding on the round bed. Jerome.

My first inclination was to run out and try to catch the cop. My second thought was to see if my Sig 9mm was still in the secret compartment of the car and use it to get even with this shmuck. I've got permits to carry, good in five states including

Virginia, but maybe the delay in shooting him would keep it from looking like self-defense. So I just looked at him for a minute or so. The guy kept trying to move, which obviously hurt him somewhere, and he was making panicky noises through the gag. Finally, I pulled out my six-inch Viper—which I'm never without—flicked open the blade, and just kept looking at him. His eyes showed he got the message. I walked toward him slowly, put the sharp point of the curved blade against his cheek, and cut through the gag, taking no care whatsoever not to scratch his face.

"Goddamn… You crazy son… I thought you were gonna cut my throat!" he almost screamed.

"Oh, shit. You mean I pulled in the wrong direction? Here… Let me try it again."

"Hey, man… Cut the crap and get me to a doctor. This thing's bleeding again."

"What's bleeding? Your back, your butt…?"

"Where she shot me, damn it!" he hollered.

"Where she… Laurel shot you?"

"Who else, damn it? The cook?"

"And just when did Laurel supposedly pop you?"

"Right after I capped you. You were on your way down, but you didn't look that bad."

"Oh, thanks. I had a surgeon up the road who had a different opinion. And it looks like I'm going to have to get you up to the hospital to get the bullet out. Not wild about you bleeding in my car."

"No bullet. She got that out."

"Must have felt good."

"Only the headache. Half a fifth of Maker's Mark inside and the outside of the bottle on the back of my head. She got the slug out of my hip, but it keeps bleeding when I sit up to piss. Think I broke a stitch or something."

"How long you been alone here?" I asked.

"Just since this morning. I think she found out you were on your way back. Hell… I don't know."

The more I thought about the last two weeks, the crazier it all felt. There was nothing pushing me now except a little bit of hunger and the thought of Jerome bleeding out while I watched. But farther into my head, there was something more. First, who the hell was this Laurel? Second, why the fuck did I have to get shot? And third, and most important, was there maybe a story here somewhere?

I didn't say anything to Jerome, simply left the room with him screaming behind me. I checked the windows around the front of the building, then the door… Saw no one. So far the only thing of value I was missing was a credit card. The laptop and everything else that should have been in my backpack were still there. Something to work with. While I gained strength, this would help.

Of course, Jerome didn't quite get it. I told him I wanted some information. I'd dropped my little recorder up in Charlottesville. If I was going to keep any of this… I can keyboard faster than I can write, and I can read it tomorrow. With a ballpoint or pencil… Forget it. Jerome didn't get any of this. Finally, I had to ask him if he ever wanted to eat again. That seemed to get his attention.

CHAPTER 3

It was all about $3.2 million of Las Vegas money. Jerome said it wasn't the amount. Some of the big places could run up more than that in a day. It was the principle of the thing. You just didn't steal from Marcus—whoever the hell he was. And that was all he was going to give me till I closed the laptop and started to leave. I knew there was more.

Painfully it started to flow. Jerome had only known of her. Lana Lawrence… She had been the business manager—not the madam, he hastened to add—at a place called The Dude Ranch. Now he decided it may have been $3.5 million. Anyway… She apparently convinced Marcus…Allen Marcus, that The Dude Ranch was old hat, out of date. Marcus was the owner of the Ranch, a couple of casinos, and one of the biggest hotels… She wanted to build a kind of mini high-rise with balconies, couple of pools... Kind of like Miami in the desert. Boss went for it. The architects, builders...they came in a little over $17 million. Nothing. But—the money had to come in—right?

"She can tell you more about the money thing than I can," he said. "I heard 'em say it was like reverse laundering—whatever the hell that is. But I heard Marcus was managing to get a lot of casino income out of the US and into Colombia through a legitimate construction company. This company was supposed to invest in The Desert Beach... They were going to call it The Desert Beach... So Marcus could use some of his money but no taxes. Of course, Marcus had to come up with his half in the open, and the Feds would be watching. Well, Miss Lana had this idea. She wanted to be made half-owner of The Dude Ranch and have Marcus sign for a legal loan against the Ranch and all the property around it for 3.5 mil that she would then invest in The Desert Beach. Marcus had trusted her with a lot of money for ten years or more. Why not? Now get me out of here! I'm sick of this fucking wet bed!"

"Hold... Hold on here a minute. How the hell did she manage to get 3.5 or 3.2 million out of Las Vegas?"

"How the hell should I know? Ask her!" he yelled

One other thing kept rattling around in my head. "Is your Mr. Marcus going to be sending any more guys like you after me?"

"Not if you get me out of here alive. 'S obvious you don't know shit. And I'll tell 'em! Just get me out of here!"

"Too fast, man. We need a story. See... I told them Jerome shot me. You'll be in deep yogurt. Where's your Glock?"

"The broad took it."

"Okay... There was another guy here that I didn't see. He shot both of us. You good with that?"

"Yeah, yeah, I'll go with that. But listen, writer, if you're getting a thing for Lana, you're just looking for more trouble. Marcus won't let his boy kill her till he finds his money. But if you're there, you're paid for. You understand what I mean?"

I thought it seemed pretty clear.

I called the police up in Roanoke. Told them what I'd found, left everything unlocked, and took off on a short road to the north that the officer said joined up with the Parkway in a mile or so. I was out of the range of Jerome's screaming, and I'd beaten the sirens.

CHAPTER 4

I stayed on the Blue Ridge Parkway all the way down to Asheville. Why not? No hurry now. I had no idea what they did to cover my spot in the seminar. Be fun to tell them, "I got shot and couldn't make it."

I had a reservation—two weeks ago—at the Palace Hotel in Asheville. They forgave me and let me check in for a few days. I wasn't sure what I wanted to do for the next three or four weeks except check the hills and valleys a few miles south, down on the end of the mountain chain. I heard about a place called the Dark Corner and that there were some valleys down there big enough to hide a battleship. Somebody sent me a book on the history of the place once. A lot of revenuers and deputy sheriffs found out that walking around through those valleys and hillsides was a good way to get a shortened life.

I walked around Asheville for a while, checked out a couple of good bookstores, and decided that the Biltmore House might be more fun with some nice lady who knew her way around the place—all ninety-five rooms of it.

I saw an ad in a little newspaper I picked up. It had a silly picture of a real estate agent down the road who sounded like he might be crazy enough to take me on a tour around the edges of the Dark Corner, looking… I don't know.

Anyway, I pulled off of I-26 onto some crazy traffic circles and found a good-sized coffee shop and bakery about a mile down the road. I'd just got comfortable with a big *mocha*—without milk—when this guy with a good tan and wearing a black suit sat down at my table. He had dark, wavy hair and almost needed a shave. He wasn't carrying a coffee.

"You looking for another *bed-and-breakfast?*" he asked. There was nothing friendly in his voice.

"Just looking around. Pretty countryside. How about you?"

"Driving around with my old man. He's in the car outside. Wants to talk to you."

I picked up the cup and took a long drink then just held the cup and looked at him.

"And leave the drink here. Come on now. Don't make me help you spill it."

I thought that if Jerome could pull a trigger on me this guy could slap my hand. So I put down the mocha, used a napkin for a blot, and pushed back from the table.

Johnny-come-nasty jumped up first and pointed to the door. "White limo under the tree," he said.

He motioned me toward the right side and held the car rear door for me. I thought that was nice. A man with a well-tanned bald head and a dark gray suit sat in the front passenger's seat. He turned so he had a full view of the back seat.

"How did you like the Mountain Laurel Lodge?" the older man on the other side of the white leather seat asked. He was a handsome older guy in a black suit, a well-aged version of the man who had just spoiled my cup of mocha.

"Well, the first few hours weren't bad, but I didn't get breakfast, and I got shot before I could pay my bill. Yeah… I've stayed in better places. Oh, and I didn't get my credit card back."

"Yes… You getting shot was regrettable. We'll need to counsel Jerome on that," the man next to me said. With all the trouble Jerome had caused recently his suit color had probably faded to a John Travolta white. "Jersey, will you take care of that."

"Certainly, sir," the man in front of me answered.

"Hey! Jerome's mine," the other man answered.

"Jersey will handle it," the older man said quietly. After a short awkward pause, he added, "Are you meeting Lana—Laurel—down here?" he asked.

"Not unless she's got her tarot cards working." Then I thought better of playing with these guys. "No. No, I'd never met the woman till that night. And after what she did to the guy to get the bullet out of his hip… I think Laurel worries me. No. No plans to meet her at all, thank you."

"Do you know why I'd like to see her?"

"The guy she operated on said something about three million bucks."

"Three-and-a-half," the younger man said from behind the wheel.

"Just so you know, I'm Allen Marcus," the man next to me said. "That's my son in front. Same name but don't call him Junior. Doesn't like it for some reason. *Al* will do."

I nodded. He didn't return the gesture.

"Lana—or Laurel—may actually have had a good idea. I don't know. But the problem was she didn't even ask me. Now three million plus is a large piece of change, don't you think? When Jerome called us with your license number, we did a little checking. You're pretty well off. Not what we call *whale* level, short of the billions, but writing's been pretty good for you. So you wouldn't be planning to go into business with the lady, would you." It was not a question.

"Mr. Marcus, I might have wanted to go to bed with the lady, but I've never had any idea of going into any kind of business with her. That sure as hell has not changed."

"Good. Good. Yes," Senior said. "Oh, one other thing. The way things are, it might be safer for you to forget about getting close enough for doing a beddy-bye with the woman. It might not be really safe. I'm sure you understand." He sat looking at me with an eyebrow raised.

"I can assure you I am not looking for her nor—"

"Look, fella," the younger Marcus said. "You only think you know this slut. You won't find her unless she wants to use you. If Lana wants you, she'll find you. I'm making book on it, so get ready."

"My son takes a somewhat negative attitude toward people he doesn't like. But he has a point." The older man extended his left hand and flicked his index finger. "Junior," he said, "give him one of your cards so if he should see Lana he can call you."

Al reacted slightly to *Junior*, but I got a card. The card had the name of one of the larger hotels in Las Vegas, a mobile phone number, and the name *Marcus*.

"If we happen to meet again," Senior said, "I hope it is in one of our hotels in Nevada. I'd be happy to entertain you as my guest."

I actually believed the smile.

There was suddenly a very solid *click* in all four doors.

"You can let yourself out," Junior said.

And I did.

The white limo spit a few pieces of gravel, wasting no time leaving the parking lot. It headed back toward the circles and I-26. Asheville, Charlotte, I didn't know and hoped I didn't need to.

I guess real estate agents have to be smiling alpha personalities, ready to take over the situation you're in and make you glad they're doing it. Jeffry Cobb had a company in a big old house just before I got into a little town called Tryon. I warned him I could be wasting his time. He laughed. I told him I didn't actually want to be in a city. He laughed and said something I didn't catch. I told him I wanted a few acres, that I didn't want to see anyone's roof or hear their TVs. He laughed again and said it sounded like I was building the heaven that every realtor wants to go home to at night. And that's the way it went till nearly dark. He offered to take me to dinner or to put me up for the night. He said that just on the edge of town was a great bed-and-breakfast, called The Lodge…

"No thanks Jeffry, but I will call you."

I didn't mention it, but I've got this shared secretarial service back in DC. This super-gal, Tina, looks after my mail and stuff. I don't really use her for communication much, but she keeps track of bills and letters from the business side of what I do. Could have called her from the hospital, but I didn't. I got back to Asheville, ate in the hotel—the food wasn't bad—went to the room and called DC. Tina chewed me out and angrily read a list of the mail I should know about. The only one she didn't think she could deal with was from Germany. The return said a kennel in Bavaria.

"Yeah, Tina… Send that one on down here. You can deal with the rest, can't you? Great. Call you back in a couple of days."

So here I was with a real estate contact down the road and three interesting story plots to think about—at least one should keep me busy through the winter. And now maybe, just maybe, the kind of deal on a Doberman pinscher I was looking for. All I had to do was keep the Marcus family and friends out of my life and… I heard three light knocks at the door.

"Housekeeping? Housekeeping? Pirrows?" a high-pitched, light, and accented voice said.

I double checked the bed from the desk. Sure enough, no pillows. I looked through the security peephole and saw a bare arm holding two king-sized pillows. I took off the safety loop, pushed down on the latch, and walked back toward the room.

"I doubt that Junior and his buddy could hear you from here, but please don't scream." Laurel or Lana held Jerome's Glock between two pillows, looking at me with a slight wise-ass smile.

Looking into the muzzle of that Glock for the second time did stop me for a moment, but after the second breath, I said, "Lady you're nuts! Junior was betting you'd come looking for me. You're gonna get us both killed."

"Well, maybe. But not tonight. They're all still with Daddy at that motel they own a piece of down the road. His jet's taking him back home in the morning. Then Junior's in charge, and we may have trouble."

"What is this *we* crap, lady? I want no piece of Marcus's money! Not a dollar!"

"Good… More for me." She smiled again.

"How do you know they don't have this floor of the hotel covered? They could be in the room across the hall!"

"Nope… No way. That's mine," she said.

I dropped down onto the foot of the bed, wondering if there might be a fire escape out the window. Here I was with this very smart but crazy woman with some handle on three million dollars that belonged to a Las Vegas equivalent of a New York *Don*. And, of course, my only role so far was to get shot. Wonderful! My 9mm Sig Sauer was hidden in my car in the valet parking garage. Trying to get to it now could be awkward and trying to walk out with Lana could become more than just awkward. So I decided I had only one way to go. Try to get the story—the real story—and find a way out.

"Why the hell don't you just Fed Ex the man back his money except for a hundred-thou or so, go live in Thailand, and help them with the elephant population? You'd be less likely to get trampled than shot."

"Could be a thought," she said, "except for one thing. I don't have anywhere near that much to give him."

"You spent over three *mil* on that lodge?" I tried to keep my voice down, but it wasn't easy.

"Hey! Had expenses, all right? But not spent, love. Invested. I had this three-and-a-half *very large* in my hand, and the thought of getting out of that fucking desert kept beating on me. For a long time I'd had this idea for a…house…*without* live-in women. Not a hotel or even a motel. Too easy to check. An actual bed-and-breakfast, but with a difference."

I started poking around in my pack for the Scotch.

"No! No booze," she said sharply. "Listen to what I'm telling you. And stay sharp now—just in case. Okay?"

I moved back to the desk chair. She sat on the bed. Enough skirt slipped up to show some great legs. She had my attention.

"It's almost like everything else—location, location, location. Needs to be on or near a tourist road and not more than an hour away from three, maybe four or five, cities of some size. Business, manufacturing, university, something. Then you build it right and advertise in the right places—the right way."

"But how do you keep the mommas and brats from running into the…guys with dolls?"

"Reservations for the lovers—always. And it's all overnight. No quick trips. For the kids looking for a sticky-bun breakfast, nothing else on the schedule? Fine. Otherwise, we're booked up. Sorry, dear."

"And just how the hell do you keep the lovers from running into each other?"

"Everything's on the cell phone. Private number for each. What you didn't see behind the lodge were six individual drive-through garages, each with a walk-out door when we open it that leads to a lovely designed rear entrance. Everything after that is room service from your private cell phone number. No kids in the house, and you've got the run of the place if you want it. And, no… It's not cheap.

"But why of all… Southern Virginia? I don't…"

"Edge of the Bible Belt and nothing obvious. Unless something has started up around the new casinos in North Carolina, there's no competition that I know of. And it's cash to start. Credit card only after we check you—and your license plate. A little Las Vegas touch there."

"You mean the states are happy to check plate numbers for you?"

"Oh no, but they're hackable—and on a commercial scale. My guess is that's how Marcus found me, by asking the hackers 'who's new?' Should have guessed."

So now I thought I had the why of the story—or at least a big part of it. How did Lana manage to work that much cash out of Nevada? I was probably no more curious than the FBI might be. But right now, I was even more curious how this evening with Laurel or Lana was going to end. Then just as I thought about possibly getting close to the woman, Jerome entered my mind.

"Jerome mentioned you performed a little surgery on his backside."

She chuckled slightly as she pointed to the carafe of water on the desk. "And the doc said some CPR probably saved my life. I guess I owe you some thanks."

"And Margarete, the cook, for keeping the pressure on…" She laughed. "After she whacked Jerome with a skillet to keep him quiet."

She sipped the water. I still wanted the Scotch.

"There's a little white cap, a gold pin, and a diploma in a storage locker somewhere. Four years to get a degree in nursing, and I went to work for a gynecologist who just happened to have the contract to look after the girls at the Ranch. We were out there one day, and I heard Marcus Senior yelling at the guy who was supposed to be the business manager of the place. One thing led to another, and a few months later, I had a nice office and a lot of numbers to deal with."

"What did you know about bookkeeping?"

"Nothing to start. But my mother was an accountant, and I got a crash course. It worked out."

Too much of this was beginning to make sense. If I wasn't careful, I could actually get comfortable with the story. I really did not want to get shot again. So what did I do? Kick the lady out? No… Wait… She had the Glock. Okay, ask her to leave? Really?

"Not to worry," she said. "I hooked up a little gadget I got at RadioShack. If they break into my room, they've got three seconds to find the switch before the horn and sirens start. We'll have the fire department, SWAT, and the National Guard here before they can make it to the elevator."

"And what if they decide to hit here first?"

"Well, if you're good, I may decide to give you the Glock."

"And what would you do? Hide in the closet?"

"I've always got my little German number, seven-six-five something. Just like 007 had in the movies. Smaller hole but hits harder than those funky things the Vegas boys are using these days. Two of us behind a mattress ought to do pretty well. You can have Jerome, but Junior is mine, okay?"

"And this other guy—Jersey?"

"Jersey'll be with Allen—Senior. That one's special. Pleasant enough, but I wouldn't mess with him."

And I was convinced she meant every word she said. Now look, I write stuff like this for fun and profit. But recently I'd been shot, and I was probably being stalked by two or three Las Vegas hard-asses. Not exactly in my job description. I doubted my publisher's insurance policy would cover crap like this.

"Come on now," she said. "Don't look so serious. I'm sure the night is free. Later on, you can say, 'We'll always have Asheville, sweetheart,' if you're into Bogart."

CHAPTER 5

Not since I was about sixteen had I felt like sex with a beautiful woman might be worth betting my life on. That night with Lana came damn close. Toward daylight, I began to wonder if the office manager of The Dude Ranch brothel might be able to monitor a few cameras—just to be certain of customer satisfaction, of course. Worth getting shot for? Hard to say, but close.

Lana wanted to shower in my place while I kept a lookout through the security peep. Reasonable Idea. She had all the artillery in the bathroom with her, but still a reasonable idea. Afterwards, I dressed, went into the hall as though I was headed for breakfast, and Lana made the dash for her own room. Since all hell did not break loose, I assumed she made it to the switch on all the bells and whistles and such.

In spite of the glow, a couple of things were digging at me. First, I had not heard any word from the lady about how she might get the three-plus mil back to Marcus or at least come to some less than fatal compromise. We had also not talked about any future plan to either get together or avoid each other. The Marcus family had been right about her finding me. But Junior's bet on her wanting something from me still bothered me. Somehow I didn't think it was sex he had in mind. So if he was right, just what the hell could I do to help her out of this mess, especially without getting myself in deeper trouble?

I picked up a copy of the *Times* and was just beginning to enjoy breakfast when the answer to the second question began to show itself. A cell phone burped inside my jacket. The short burp indicated a message. Okay. The only trouble was the noise this phone made was not the same as mine. I fished the unit from my pocket.

"Yours is in the bathroom cabinet. Check it."

I don't know where the lady learned her light-finger techniques, but I'd like to take some lessons. My cell was right where she said, and there was a message.

"Tell Marcus SENIOR I want to talk to him. See what we can work out. Forget the mil, but a nice deed, instead."

Now, the number on the card I had didn't say whose it was, but I would have bet it was Junior's. It was. And, no, he would not give me his father's.

"Old man gave me—*me*—the bitch and finding the money or what's left of it. She can talk to me now—or wait till I find her, then I don't think we'll talk much."

"Well, ah… Al… She didn't answer when I tried to call back. When she calls back or texts do I give her your number?"

"Fucking A… I don't care how much she's got left. You don't steal from Marcus. Fact is you don't steal from Vegas. Sets a bad example. She knows that. Only thing she can do now is leave whatever she's got left and get to the moon."

"Or Thailand."

"Where?"

"Oh… Nowhere. Just an old movie we were talking about at the lodge the night before Jerome shot me. Nowhere, really." I hoped he bought that.

"Whatever… You give her this number and *you* call me back." And he clicked off.

I couldn't resist checking the room across the hall. The housekeeping ladies were hard at work, and there were no personal items left. Where did she go? No idea. What was she driving? Not a clue. I quickly checked. I had my valet ticket and my other key. She'd probably found a Mercedes. But where *might* she go? Now there was something to think seriously about.

If I was going to be the communications hub, a job I really did not want, I had to put myself in the center of the circle. I needed a big map here, and where were the prop-guys on the movie set when you needed them? She knew who and what to watch out for, so staying in Asheville could make sense. It was a fairly short road trip back to Mountain Laurel Lodge, but that was probably covered by the local law as well as Marcus. Very few really long flights out of the Asheville airport, and the larger Charlotte terminal was a couple of hours away. And from Charlotte, she'd go where and why? Back to square one—almost. The lady obviously knew she'd run into Junior trying to get to Papa by phone. Surely even Jerome was smart enough to cover any airline reservations from Asheville to Vegas via Charlotte or Atlanta. Could she have chartered a jet? That would spend a lot more of her loot. Maybe rent a local car and just head west? That might work. But if Senior or Junior wanted to see her quick… That could be a problem. Yeah…square one. If I had to bet, I'd guess she was still in Asheville or damn close.

I hung the *do not disturb* sign on the door and tried to take a nap to catch up. Lana's Dior on the sheets didn't let that happen. I strolled over to the bookstore with the coffee-bar. Two milk-less mochas and more thinking—or plotting—or planning. Whatever it was, it didn't feel very useful. Then a short text on my own cell. "Indian restaurant for lunch."

I found a neat and great-smelling Indian restaurant on a street behind the hotel. I had no idea what the menu was talking about, so when something passed that looked good I pointed to it. Halfway into enjoying it, I got a long ring. Lana.

"Betting that Junior said no," she said.

"Right again, Miss Sunshine," I replied.

"Don't look for me. If you see me, don't show it. Got a plan. Little dancing. Just stay loose." She clicked off. That was it.

Wish I knew what I was eating.

Back in my room at 2:30 or so, I got a call from Junior.

"Thought I told you to call if you heard from her."

"You did, but I left your card on the desk, and I was eating out. When I let her know you were the only one she could talk to, she hung up on me. Didn't seem to want to talk. Nothing more I can tell you."

Junior clicked off.

I couldn't help but wonder what these two would do if I suddenly checked out and cancelled my cell phone service. Then it only got worse. About an hour later, I got a call from Jeffry Cobb, the realtor.

"You didn't tell me your wife was with you." He continued without pausing. "She wanted to see if there was a nice inn or B and B, so I showed her the inn up near the center of town, and I think she checked in. Did you forget we had an appointment this afternoon?"

I waited a moment to see if he'd stopped then assured him I was to call him when my business situation eased off. He talked on for a while, but I had no idea what he was saying.

So now Lana was complicating the picture with a little town that was fifty miles away and just about as hard to get to as the Mountain Laurel. Or maybe this was not a complicating factor. The town map that Cobb had given me showed only about a half dozen streets running cross-hatch through a circle. There were a lot of sidewalk benches and second- and third-story windows for watching. Any movement through the place should be obvious. Maybe the lady had a plan. I just wished I knew what it was. And then there was something else.

Laurel Landry, Lana Lawrence… We were into alliterations here. So was my new *wife's* first name Donna? Or Deloris? Oh, please… Anything but Daisy.

Lana had blocked the numbers from the phones she used to call me. I wanted to find out how to save my ass in any grand plan connected with this move to Tryon. I did not relish the idea of calling the Medford Inn and asking for *my wife*. Now it wasn't that there hadn't been some chances, some really nice chances in fact. But it always seemed like I was up to my nuts in some deadline or dashing off to a movie set in some crazy place when I had a screenwriting job, or taking off to learn more about some crime or terrorist activity. And then I thought about the best age to have kids, and whatever it was, I had to be past it. For me that was probably twenty-one. So asking for *the misses* was not a comfortable thing for me.

"Oh…hi," the lady said. "This is Monica. Your wife ran out over two hours ago. She said, if you called, she'd call you later, and you could decide where to eat. I told her we could fix you a dinner here… Beef, salmon, veggies, whatever—"

I tried to cut her off. "Monica, she said something about…Spartanburg I think. Not sure. One of us will call you back. But thanks." I rang off.

Making the trip out of Asheville down I-26 to the crazy circles that led to the Tryon road was getting boring. I passed Jeffry Cobb's place and drove around the town till I found the Medford Inn. Then I thought I'd look around for a restaurant possibly within walking distance of the Medford where we wouldn't be too obvious. Heading out, on the edge of this little town, I saw a hill on the right side of the road that went up about fifty feet. A paved driveway had been cut into the side, and at the top a large house had been made into a Masonic lodge. If the gentlemen weren't having a meeting tonight, it looked like a good place to watch from.

I'd been up there about half an hour when this black SUV with tinted windows turned into the driveway. Then it hit me that there was no other road off the hill. This had to be Jerome or Junior. The black bus pulled up with the driver's door right in front of me. I ducked down, hit the hidden latch, and the armrest came open at the bottom. I could get a grip on the Sig with no trouble. I slowly looked through the steering wheel and saw Lana smiling at me through the lowered window. She drove on around so we were door-to-door.

"I got burgers," she said, "but there's a pizza place up the street a way."

We drove around and parked a bit more respectably, like we were waiting for a meeting. She had followed me halfway down from Asheville, just to see if Junior or Jerome was following me—or her.

"Where did you get the SUV?"

"A loaner. Don't ask."

"Okay. But there's one thing I gotta ask. Why the hell this wife bit in Tryon?"

She put some mustard on her second burger. "Well, this gets a little funky, but it already seems to be working." She took a big bite. "I got Monica at the inn to do a 411 call on the hotel in Vegas, Al Senior's office, to see if your credit card was still good. Of course, I didn't get Marcus but two secretaries and then—ta-da, Jersey. Told him I would only talk to the boss, but if he wanted me to work with him—Jersey—I could do that, but not Junior. Otherwise, I was off to India or Thailand or somewhere."

"And…?"

Lana chewed on the burger then slurped quite a lot of Coke. "And nothing till noon tomorrow. Meanwhile, he called Junior to stand down, he said. I think that means he is to lay off."

"You believe he will?"

"Hell no," she said, still munching the burger. "But I think he'll be very damn careful what he does if Papa or Jersey tells him to be nice."

I felt relaxed enough for my second burger. There was one really big problem here. Not only did I not have even a modicum of control over what was going on, I had no real value at stake, except perhaps a storyline, and I was being dragged along by my hormones. Oh, I'd been pulled into tough spots by my crotch before, but I always had something more invested. And, yes, I did have some skin in this game as they say, but this time the skin was just that—skin. Maybe if I knew a little more of…anything.

"So just who the hell is this *Jersey*, really?"

"Good question," she answered. "Lot of it is rumor. But one day, few years back, he shows up in a marine uniform with a bunch of stripes and his arm in a sling. Passed a card to the line of secretaries and watchdogs, and finally, Marcus saw him. A month or so later, he was back in a well-tailored suit and no sling. Marcus Senior is the only one he talks to. Six months later, he's listed as assistant manager of operations."

"What the hell does that mean?"

"Turns out it means the operation of everything. No one says *no* to Jersey. And he's kind of a body-guard. Where the boss is, Jersey is. Of course, Junior hates his living guts."

"That was obvious when I first met 'em. Who's gonna shoot who first?"

"I wouldn't bet against Jersey whether it was bullets or battleaxes. I've always had the feeling the big guy's been there and back."

"Junior doesn't see that?"

"Junior only sees the name on the door. He's a Marcus. He's untouchable."

"Papa agree with that?"

"You saw them together. What do you think?"

CHAPTER 6

The *missus* didn't seem to object when Monica handed me both keys. Monica asked if we wanted help getting our things up the flight of stairs. There wasn't that much really. *My wife* had a backpack and a soft duffel, and I had a pack and a suit bag. No problem.

The Medford Inn was comfortable enough, and I guess you'd have to say it was more than nice. It was different from the Howard Johnson style of everything that took over a few decades ago and it made you stop and think for a minute. The room was big enough for the queen-sized bed, small table and two chairs, and single chest with vanity but it had no room for you to practice your tango steps. The closet was shallow but workable, and the old-fashioned bathroom had a shower over the tub.

It all worked well, and it was totally comfortable, just…different.

My *wife*—damned if I was going to call her Darla… Anyway, the woman in the room with me seemed to think this was all fun. Fact is, she made it that way. The bed did not squeak. The inlaid wooden floor under a simple rug did not squeak either—as far as we could tell, the non-engineered lodging was as good as it had to be.

Breakfast and a total oral report on the local news from Monica made trying to read the little local paper both impossible and needless. There was one other table in use by a mom and pop with two rather noisy kids whose working vocabulary seemed centered around the words 'I want…' I thought Monica concentrating on us was perhaps understandable. Into our second coffee, she came from the kitchen with a note. It was from Jeffry Cobb. I had scheduled a meeting with him for 9:30. He was just checking.

Catching the fresh air of the early autumn morning over sips of my third coffee almost made me forget the problem I was now connected to with *my wife*. I tried to tell her that staying in the same bed on consecutive nights could be dangerous—too easy for Junior to track. For some reason, she didn't seem too concerned. She gave me a perfunctory agreement, said she'd check herself out and contact me later on the mobile. I thought I ought to probe at least a little in case… I really wasn't sure what the *case* might be. How could I help her, except maybe to tell her to run? Then again, the case might be to protect myself. My gut told me this whole thing was getting way out of control. But the Marcus family had me tied into their three-plus million dollar search for Lana, and it seemed like I could either help her or run and hide myself.

All she said to me was, "Got to find a good law firm in Virginia. Later…"

As I drove into the floral-landscaped parking area facing the old mansion Cobb or someone was refurbishing, a white SUV stopped right behind my car, leaving just room enough for the driver's door to fully open. Junior. I said nothing. Let him set the stage and lead. I'd counter-punch. I rolled down my window. He leaned against the door.

"Amazing what you can find in a guy's room when the maid's using the vac with headphones on her ears."

"I could have told you about the realtor here last week when I met your father and Mister Jersey."

Junior jerked his head slightly when I said *Mister Jersey*. Obviously, I knew who the man was now.

"Yes, but it's a lot more fun finding all your notes scribbled on this funny little thing they call a newspaper. Only thing I don't see is Lana's cell number. Why don't you give it to me easy like?"

I wasn't sure how far I could get away with pushing this, but I had to let him know we were aware of the new limits. "I can give you the only number I know, and I don't think she'll answer. The last I heard from her, she had a new burner cell and number for some office in Vegas. Maybe if you call home, they'll give it to you."

There was certainly a possibility he might have slammed his fist through the open window, but my right hand was on the ledge, my left on the latch. While I don't look as formidable as Jersey, I do try to stay in shape, and I've done several years of martial arts and self-defense training. If Papa really checked on me, he probably knew that. Junior could have lost a right elbow, had the corner of the door in his face, and knees were optional. He dropped the little newspaper thing on the ground and walked away with a sneer.

Jeffry Cobb waited until the white SUV was totally out of the parking lot and headed back toward I-26 before he opened the office door. He walked out to meet me with a rather apprehensive look, as though he wanted to make sure there wasn't another Junior around.

Jeffry was showing me copies of surveyors' plats of everything from two to twenty acres. He kept trying to push me higher, so I could have a horse farm. I finally had to tell him that if he mentioned *horse* one more time, I was leaving. He got the idea. He had aerial photographs of some of these places. A couple of parcels in the ten- to fifteen-acre range seemed interesting and fairly isolated. One was a triangular ridge at the end of a road about five miles out of the northwest side of Tryon. It looked like it had about half a house on the edge of a bluff with a stream or little river at the bottom. That was definitely on my list to see.

While we were driving the twisting up and down blacktop roads, and I was trying to tune out Jeffry's constant chatter about people and happenings in three counties, something hit me that should have been a discussion item between Lana and me days ago. And it was something I knew nothing about.

"Jeffry, is there any gambling in the Carolinas? I mean like casino gambling?"

"Only one that I know of. A really nice place up the road fifty or sixty miles. Place called Cherokee. It's on Indian land, but it operates just like big places in Atlantic City or Las Vegas. You would not believe the screaming from the church groups. Took some sort of federal action for the tribe to finally get it approved, but the screaming still went on. Been up there a few times. Really nice. Great food, and they've got parks for the kids if mamma won't leave them at home."

"Anything in South Carolina?"

"Not that I know of. Too bad. Myrtle Beach would be an ideal place year round."

"How about Virginia?"

"No idea. Little outside my range of operations."

Now I'd been living in Virginia, little place called The Plains, for almost five years. I'm far enough west of DC to avoid a lot of the political noise but still get copies of the *Post* and *The Wall Street Journal* every morning. If Indian casinos had been an issue in Virginia, it must have shown up in the state section of the *Post*, which I rarely paid any attention to. I was beginning to think I'd been missing something very important here. I called Tina.

"Where the hell have you been for the last two years?" she asked. "Virginia and South Carolina seem to be about the only states on the coast without a casino or two owned or operated by Indians on some bit of old reservation land."

"Tina my love, here's why I pay you the big bucks. Get a hold of the *Post*'s morgue keeper and get everything you can on casinos in Virginia for the past two years. Make a copy for our files, and then send 'em all to my laptop. This isn't just for fun, lady. This could even…"

She clicked off on me. Now a stranger to my world might think this was just an impolite way for Tina to reject my order—or request. Not so. Tina understood what I wanted. Why fuss around with meaningless goodbyes or whatever? That was Tina.

Bits of things from my first evening with Laurel—Lana—had been creeping in and out of my consciousness for days. Nevada, Nevada, Nevada… The furnishings from a remodeled Reno hotel, the mention of casinos when she finally got around to telling me what the Mountain Laurel Lodge was supposed to be, and her insistence on holding on to both the money and the lodge, and talking to Marcus Senior. And something she said made it seem as though she was uncertain about the title to the land the building was on. The 'ifs' and 'maybes' were beginning to keep me from thinking really clearly about anything, including my own safety. And one of the things that really began to pound on me was Marcus Junior. Was he several steps ahead of me on this? Did he think—perhaps correctly—that Lana was maybe way ahead of any possible competition if an Indian-owned casino could be approved in Virginia? Was he more interested in keeping the idea of the money in front of his father but *really* after whatever paper Lana held on the land—just in case?

So I waited. Back at the inn, a brief call with Jeffry told me more about all the weird and wonderful people he knew—people I hoped I'd never have to meet—and I also found that *Darla* had not checked out of the Medford Inn or returned. The inn had its own Wi-Fi, so why not take advantage of its dining room and have a quiet evening without the anxious moments that being near Lana was creating? I didn't expect Tina to stay up all night watching

Indian-casino news, even though her office was part of her home, a remodeled townhouse just off Connecticut Avenue. Still… So after creating a document file with all the inconsistencies I'd accumulated in Lana's tales and half lies, I propped up on the bed and quickly fell asleep watching the usual next to nothing on TV.

CHAPTER 7

My watch said it was 7:44 when the house telephone next to the bed forced me out of a restful sleep. Monica apologized almost frantically for possibly awakening me. She assured me that Darla had sworn I always woke early. The point of it all was that I had apparently allowed my cell phone's battery to run down, and she had been unable to call me. Monica was simply to tell me that Darla was visiting Mrs. Lincoln. She was assured I would know what that meant. Happily, Monica decided to stay in the game.

"Isn't that one of Carl Sandburg's books?" she asked. Without waiting for an answer, she continued. "His home is just up the road, almost in Hendersonville. Flat Rock, I think."

Not much of a cryptic cipher, but I'm sure it would have Junior parked and guessing. If Lana was in Flat Rock, I'd have to think about driving up there. Was there a reason to? Yep, I'd have to think about it. But something else demanded my attention first. I sat combing through thirty-eight pages of copy from the *Post* on the multi-sided casino battle between several Indian tribes in the Commonwealth of Virginia and their opponents. The tribes and the organizations that supported their use of casino gambling to achieve financial independence and support higher education were being challenged by several groups, including a large hotel casino in Maryland that did not want the competition. And it didn't take me long to find that the semi-sane ultra-conservative legislature had kept a casino bill bottled up in committee for five years.

I wonder if all politicians wear Kevlar on a daily basis.

I may not be the fastest reader on the planet, but I was surprised at how long it took me to digest all the legalese in the material Tina sent me. I was making a couple of notes here and there when I found something that might fit with what I thought Lana was getting into. And I couldn't help but wonder if she actually knew all the crap she was wading into if I was right. It took me the better part of the morning to read all the stuff from the *Post* and to type a couple of pages making sense out of my notes. The very kind Monica let me make some printouts for Lana.

There was one more thing I needed from Monica. Would she please, *please*, tell no one that the lovely Darla had called and had spent the night elsewhere? I told her it concerned a family business problem and that some unpleasant gentlemen were trying to get her to sign over some real estate. Her eyes got a little wider with every word, and she was nodding in agreement before I finished. It has always amazed me how eager most people are to be involved in any sort of conspiracy until they look down the barrel of a pistol and consider they may be on the wrong side.

A phone conversation with Jeffry Cobb on the *why* of a possible return visit by Junior Marcus really didn't appeal to me. I decided to take a chance. If he hadn't been there, great. If he had… Well, I'd learned that walking toward the door was a good way to push Jeffry's off-button.

The fifteen or so acres on the high bluff continued to interest me. There was an unfinished house that

I really didn't give a rat's ass about, and apparently, no one else did either. It had some sort of wild story, and it seemed there was no price on the place at the moment. But Cobb had inside information that the place would likely come up for a bankruptcy auction in the next three to six months. Or... And now I was hearing a conspiracy... Or if I made the probable amount of cash available to him—and signed the right papers of authority—he just might be able to buy out the creditors and county tax office and save everyone a lot of legal fees. Considering that no one in their right mind would even try to ride a horse up there, the price per acre did not seem excessive. I wrote him a check for 16 percent of that figure, signed half a dozen papers I sort of read, and belatedly wondered if this was really the place I wanted to get away to. Suddenly thinking about Junior, Jerome, and company, I also belatedly wondered if I'd have a chance to find out.

As I was leaving, I said I might want to see the Sandburg house in Flat Rock. Jeffry came up with a map that showed a winding secondary road, US 176.

"Lots of ups and downs and switchbacks," he said, "but it's a pretty drive, especially this time of year. Sure beats weaving your way through the semis on I-26."

He was right.

I had no idea where Lana was staying. I drove around the town, looking at the neighborhoods. Figured she'd recognize the bronze Audi two-door. And, yes, I saw half a dozen black SUVs. I passed a coffee shop and bakery sign for the second time and decided to wait in some degree of gastronomical comfort for the lady to find me. It didn't take long. She'd been parked in the driveway of an empty house about a block away. Made sense. We tried to make our meeting seem as expected and casual as possible. She got a funny sounding latté but ignored the baked delights. When she sat down, I said nothing, just laid the pages from the printer in front of her.

Lana seemed only mildly surprised at my gift. She read the heading and maybe the first sentence then chuckled. She leaned forward, close enough to whisper. "Guilty as charged," she said. "But what took you so long?"

I looked at her broad and mocking smile. "Because I really didn't want to get mixed up in any of your troubles." It was difficult to say that in a whisper.

"Oh… And here I thought you were my knight in a shining Audi come to rescue me from the wicked mobsters of the west. Oh, dear me... What must I do now?"

Unfortunately, Lana's search for a little girl's voice was loud enough to be heard beyond our table. I tried to cover it with a laugh. Not sure I'm that good an actor. I stood, picked up the double mocha, and reluctantly decided to leave most of the delicious apple turnover. Lana slowly followed my lead, and cups in hand, we made it into the parking lot without anyone placing a 911 call. The boxy black SUV was gone. She curled her empty hand through my left arm and led me toward a trim burgundy SUV with tinted windows. I didn't ask.

We drove around the neighborhood for a few minutes. I wasn't sure I could find the way back to the bakery without getting to the main road through town. A *for sale* sign between a walkway and a driveway leading to a carport brought us into a hard left turn, a rather neat 180-degree controlled spin, actually, and we parked in front of the house. With the ornate front security light, we would be able to see adequately for an hour or so in semi-safety.

"I guess I only half-lied to you." That was a comforting way for her to start. "It's mostly what I didn't tell you... At first I thought that what you didn't know might keep you out of trouble—even after Jerome... Well, that obviously didn't work. I knew that Allen Senior had ordered Junior to leave you alone. I guess we're finding out that Junior's head has gotten too big to be bossed around even by Papa."

"Whoa, wait here a minute! Sounds like you've been in touch with Marcus Senior all along."

"Shortly after I got to Asheville. A gal I know from The Dude Ranch managed to get word to him that Junior didn't intercept. And, Lover Man, that's been the big trouble for months. Junior wanted me out of the Ranch, fought the idea of The Desert Beach, and somehow found out what I was trying to set up in Virginia."

"So that lodge thing, your bordello-bed-and-breakfast, was all a sham."

"No! No, it was just like I said. It could run hot or cold."

"And Senior knew about this but not Junior?"

"Right."

"But if Jerome found you. Junior had to be close behind. And the two or three million..."

"There never was a three-million-dollar bag. Everything I bought in Virginia was paid for bank-to-bank over Allen Marcus's signature. The three-million-dollar thing was all Junior's idea to get Jerome and one of his buddies from another big casino to come to Virginia. Before he left, he mentioned a name too close to Jersey's sharp ears. It was a piece of muscle that Jersey knew worked for another casino. It's very hard to keep a secret in Las Vegas. It didn't take long for Jersey to find out that Junior was planning to set up his own organization in Virginia on the back of whatever I'd started for Papa. Of course, he had to keep the idea of the three million alive to keep his crew together. And he needed the paper on the Mountain Laurel to have some working capital. Since the state is still fighting itself over casinos on Indian land, Allen thinks he's just about out of time and likely to do something serious—and stupid. He knows his son."

If I'd been sitting in the driver's seat I might have shoved Lana out the passenger's door and taken off for one of those bootlegger valleys in the Dark Corner until all this Las Vegas casino crap blew over. Of course, I couldn't, but the thought occurred to me. And I still had some questions.

"Lady, from the stuff I got out of the clipping files, the Indian casino thing probably will happen in Virginia, but God knows when, and the different tribes, the different reservations, the land trusts…

Even when the *white man* finally says yes, the Indians still have some big decisions to make. I guess I'm not sure I see what your fancy lodge is going to do for you—or Marcus."

"You saw Margarete, the cook, the morning you met Jerome. Right?"

"Right. Good looking woman. With the tan complexion, I wondered if… Oh please. Don't tell me…"

"Margarete Wings is a full-blooded… Well, there was a white woman mixed in three or four generations back, but the rest of the tribe don't seem to care. Margarete got a scholarship and graduated with a degree in business from Virginia State. Her tribe is clustered around forty-two acres that is still reservation land, and about ten times that much trust land that their ignorance of our laws let them more or less lose about a hundred years ago. Margarete studied all this mess in college, and when she came back home, some near idiot saw the hill and all the laurel bushes and thought it would be a good place for a B and B—near enough to the Parkway and some beautiful views to the north. Margarete found a smart lawyer, and the builders put up a building they could own on land they could not. When they weren't getting enough business and wanted to add

a kiddy park and some sort of gift shop and con-
venience store, Margarete—and the tribe—said no.
The fund source, who didn't know about the land
limitations, pulled their money and… Well, that's
where I got in.

"Margarete and I got along from the start. When
I mentioned a possible casino, I didn't know whether
I was being readied for ritual assassination or corona-
tion. Seemed they all knew what the Cherokee had
been able to pull off in North Carolina. They wanted
the same thing, and I guess almost everyone they
knew was for it. But getting the money for lawyers
and public affairs work… I had some difficult days,
but Margarete understood how I was trying to make
it all work and… So here we are. Until Junior butted
in, it was slow but positive. Now…"

I hadn't seen the car pull up behind us.

CHAPTER 8

I heard a metallic double rap as Jersey's large gold ring tapped on the window. I rolled down the window—halfway.

"Mister Marcus would like to speak to you." Jersey nodded toward the dark silver four-door Lincoln that had stopped behind me. It was nothing special.

I got out, and he walked me to the rear door on the passenger's side. He gave me an efficient pat-down and opened the door. Allen Marcus Senior seemed to be relaxed. He extended his hand and gripped mine firmly. It felt sincere.

"Would I be correct in assuming that dear Lana has filled you in on the true reason for our interest in the Old Dominion State?"

"Well, the possible casino side of things seems pretty obvious. You and the Indians want 'em. The holier than anybody politicians are fighting it. And I can't say I understand all the legalese connected with land trusts and reservations, but…it seems that Lana has her lovely foot in the door with that… lodge-thing. But…" I had to stop here. I wasn't sure how to get into the family thing—or if I should. I began to feel even less secure when I looked up and saw Lana's car driving away.

"And you're wondering why I let Junior's lie, the charade about the three-and-a-half million dollars go on long enough to get you shot. Yes, you have a right to wonder and be angry. And then I wasn't completely truthful with you during our meeting at your coffee shop. I knew my son would try to follow both of you. As usual, not too smart. Jersey had already removed the agent from the other hotel, and Jerome was…sent away, so he didn't have much help I'm afraid. Would you like a Scotch and soda? We have a small bar here."

I'd only had half an apple turnover since breakfast, but the Scotch smelled expensive. A small, quick splash of soda to crack it… How could I resist? I'd take the interstate back south. Straighter. Marcus took one, then a second swallow, and settled back in the seat. He looked comfortable but not happy.

"It seemed for a while that Allen Junior had begun to believe his own lie about the three million dollars. Then as we interrogated Jerome, we discovered that he had learned about the importance of the location of the lodge and its connection with a certain tribe. How he found out about that, God only knows. But if he talked to anyone in the area, they could have told him it was on Indian land. After that…" He took another hit of the Scotch. "All the legal and financial paperwork lists Lana Lawrence as the owner of record on the trust documents and myself as her beneficiary. When we set it all up, we thought that would be protection enough." He looked down into his glass. "That was before we learned that my son had gone over…had gone to work for one of my biggest competitors in Nevada."

Allen Marcus did not hide his unhappiness in the loss of trust in his oldest son. He poured another Scotch, straight.

"And then there is the other piece of the scheme that we learned from Jerome. It seems my *friends* in Vegas did not know about the three-million-dollar lie and that Junior has no intention of cutting them in on the tribal agreement if—*if*—the casino bill is ever approved."

I had been able to keep the crazy ins and outs of this thing pretty much together. At first I wondered mostly about my own safety and how I could put some serious distance between me and these people. Then something else hit me, and I had to ask.

"Marcus, if I've got this right, Lana is probably target-one, and I become collateral damage just by being around. And then you become target number two because your name is on the paper. Is that about right?"

"Since Junior is my oldest son, you could flip the numbers, but yes, that is about right."

"And that makes Junior the next target if he really is cutting out your friends in Nevada."

"A reasonable assumption, my friend. And that is why I've told you the…problem or whatever it is. I would like for you to help protect Lana while we set a trap for my son."

"You plan to take him back to Las Vegas?"

"Indeed."

"You people in the casino business have your own court system?"

"That's a bit beyond your need to know, I'm afraid. What you do need to know is that you must protect Lana—and yourself—with the utmost care for the next forty-eight hours. You have a weapon available I assume."

"Yeah, a Sig Sauer—9mm. But I'm not…"

"And I'm sure you have a permit to carry. And Lana will always have the Walther. That should offer a bit of protection. You should be just fine."

"Look, Marcus… I get some range practice about every month, but I don't want to kill anybody. I write about it but…"

"Not to worry, my friend. I really don't think you'll have to. Just want to make sure you have some protection—just in case." Allen Marcus Senior took a healthy swallow of Scotch. "Jersey, I think we can take the gentleman back to his car now."

CHAPTER 9

And I did take the interstate back south toward Tryon. It wasn't because of the single Scotch I had with Marcus. It was to think about what I'd heard and not have to worry about the next blind switchback on that secondary road. And it was getting dark.

I hadn't checked out of the Medford Inn and the leather suit bag was still in the closet. And, yes, it did occur to me that Junior could have the place easily covered and that walking up the steps onto the porch would make me an easy target. The only comforting thought was that Senior had agreed with me about collateral damage. If I wasn't standing next to the lovely Lana... And then I had to add sitting or lying next to her. No... It was now not so comforting. And just how the hell was I supposed to protect the lady?

There was a no-parking space at the end of the walk that leads up to the porch of the Medford with flat-parking on either side of it. The inn was on my right, and I was lucky. Someone was leaving the space just before the walkway. The custom latch on the armrest worked silently, and it swung out a couple of inches, letting me get the butt of the Sig. I checked its clip and chamber, made sure of the safety, and slid it into my waistband. The extra clip didn't seem necessary, but I'd never let a character leave home without it.

Monica Dolan was her usual smiling self. She popped up from behind the desk to tell me just what I didn't really want to hear.

"Your wife beat you in," she said with a laugh. "She's already ordered dinner, and we'll be serving in about forty minutes. Is that alright?"

I assured her it was just fine.

For some reason, my legs felt a bit tired and heavy on the steps to the second floor. I told myself it was from too many hours on the road with Jeffry Cobb, and everything with this Lana…thing and, of course, dodging Junior. Yeah, part of it I'm sure. But I was fighting the idea that something in my head was talking to me physically. Maybe it was a holdover from Jerome's slug in my right chest. Maybe it was Junior's earlier warning to keep away from Lana. Maybe it was the fact that Marcus Senior had said he had a plan but didn't tell me what it was. Then he said I was to protect myself and Lana. There had been a certain emphasis in the way he added her name.

I was getting a feeling here that I really didn't like.

I write crap that is bloodier than this all the time. There's always this wise guy chasing some broad or a purse of diamonds or box of gold bars or some terrorist. He may get shot but only grazed. In the end, he gets the broad and a few bucks, and Interpol is scratching its butt wondering what happened. Why the hell couldn't I feel like the wise guy? Shit!

I got to the room door, expecting to hear the TV. Nothing. I knocked a couple of times and put the key in the lock. I walked into what almost seemed an empty room.

"Hello, husband dear." Of course it was Lana. She stood behind the door with a shiny black pistol—the Walther that Marcus had mentioned.

Now any of my characters would have looked through the hinge-crack of the partially opened door before walking in and finding a gun in their back. I've simply got to start acting like I write.

"Had a chat with Allen on the phone while you were driving down," she said. "I guess we do nothing till we hear from him—or Jersey. So in the meantime, let's eat, have a little wine, and…whatever. So, why don't you go ahead and shower? I think we ought to dress for dinner."

I decided to take her suggestion. The walls of the shower were wet—and still warm. I guess the lady had the evening planned well ahead of my arrival. How very usual.

The dining room of the Medford Inn was larger than I thought a place with only fifteen or sixteen rooms would need. It wasn't long before I found out why. Couples and families began drifting in through the front door, celebrating anniversaries, birthdays, date-night, whatever. The kitchen seemed to be a big draw. Lana and I arrived just in time to find a table that wasn't exposed in the broad wing that held the dining room and the long row of windows across the front. Somehow, I didn't figure Junior for a sniper-shot through a crowd, but I had to start trying to think defensively. And that became harder to do as the table service began. The goblets next to the water glasses held a blush wine by the time I had spread the napkin in my lap. I had no idea what Lana had ordered, but soon I was looking at a neat presentation of salmon on a bed of rice, surrounded by bits of most of the vegetables on the health charts and thin strips of very lean beef—beautiful and seasoned perfectly. I'd only had that half an apple turnover to eat since breakfast and inhaled everything on the plate down to the last grain of rice. The coffee mostly neutralized the wine but not completely. It was after 10 o'clock before we started back upstairs. The dining room was all but empty.

From the first time I saw Lana—then Laurel—I couldn't ignore the physical attraction. Even with all the craziness and lies, and getting shot, I couldn't get her out of my mind. Lovely, sexy…yes, and smart. No—more than just smart. She was intelligent and smart. She had to be to have created all this mess and lived through it—at least so far. And then the night in Ashville… Our first—actually only night here in the Medford Inn—had been

more for comforting and warmth and not unin-
hibited sex. For a moment or two, I wondered
hopefully about tonight but knew that with what
we were likely facing, it wouldn't happen, couldn't
happen.

The lady had looked special tonight. I could happily have taken her to dinner at any good restaurant
I'd ever known. This made what I was afraid might
be ahead of us all the more infuriating.

Lana came out of the bathroom in a bra and half-
slip, holding the very special dress. She spread it on
the bed, carefully folded it, and put it in the bag that
I had earlier thought was carrying the millions that
never were. She removed the half-slip, revealing the
pantyhose that she left on. Pantyhose have always
been a bit of a turn-off for me. But for Lana tonight,
it made sense. A thin long-sleeved sweater, Levi's,
flats, and I guess she was ready. Wrong again. She
spread a lightweight raincoat and a carefully folded
bundle out on the bed. It was the frilly hostess apron
I had seen that first night at the Mountain Laurel
Lodge. She saw my expression.

"Kevlar," she said. "Jersey had it made special. He
said if I ever had to fix breakfast for customers at

the lodge, I'd probably need it. I never leave home without it."

I hung up the suit, stowed the shaving gear, and got into a pair of jeans and a polo shirt. I'm sure Lana wasn't watching me as closely as I had watched her. I remembered that in my backpack I had a belt-clip holster that fit the Sig Sauer. It wasn't the best for a quick draw, but it held the pistol safely and didn't show even under the new leather jacket I'd bought to replace the one Jerome had ruined.

I leaned back on the bed, made certain my cell was charged. I looked at Lana, raised an eyebrow, and spread my arms. She smiled and gently climbed over me and into the crook of my left arm. And there we lay.

CHAPTER 10

Lana was comfortable in my arm and on my chest. We cuddled, said very little, and could have measured time by our heartbeats. We may have dozed though we tried not to. A little past five o'clock, Lana's phone started its classical signal. She put it on speaker. It was Jersey.

"Someone in Vegas told Junior he's in trouble out there. Sounds like he's gone totally *ape*. Get out now! No bags, no lights, just leave. Head south. We'll call." And that was it.

Lana slipped the wide bodice of the special apron over her head, tied the lower part around her waist, and pulled the light coat over it all. She checked the Walther in the coat pocket. Walking around the bed to the door, I slid the Sig into the holster and got into the leather jacket. We met at the door. Lana gave me a quick kiss and stepped into the dimly lit hall. Jersey had said no lights, so quietly sneaking out of the place seemed like a good idea. The bolt and chain on the heavy front door gave me a little problem, and I'm damn sure that if dear Monica slept on the ground floor of the place she could have heard us.

As quietly as we could, we made it over the eight feet or so of porch, down the two broad steps, and headed down the walk past the huge old oak tree and the steps that led to the sidewalk and the street. We made it to the steps when a black car parked on the other side of the street pulled out with a screech and sped toward us.

I was trying to pull Lana back to the tree when I heard the gun and felt the slug burn through the skin over the ribs halfway down my chest under my right arm. A second shot came from the car followed by a series of double-taps from our left, the other side of the oak. The black car sped up and then crashed right into the side of the Audi.

Lana was sliding out from my left arm and down the side of the tree. "Damn that hurt," she said. She held her chest with both hands, just below her breasts. "Kevlar or no, that smarts!"

I couldn't tell if she was injured or just pissed. Then another hand appeared and pulled Lana's away. He dug the slug out of the Kevlar apron.

"No blood," Jersey said. "Bruises heal." Then he looked at me. "Give me your Sig," he said. He held out a Walther partially wrapped in a handkerchief. "You're wounded. Easier story to work. Hurry."

It hurt my ribs to pull the Sig from the holster, but I managed. The Walther was hot. Jersey rubbed his hand and wrist over my own, dropped a full magazine in my lap, then turned to look back toward the street.

"Pretty good shooting for a writer," he said, then disappeared around the far side of the inn.

By now there were lights, lots of lights. The lights over the end steps clearly illuminated the smashed vehicles and the dead man at the wheel. It was Junior. No doubt about that. Who called the cops, I don't know, but I'd bet on Monica. The police department isn't too far from the inn, and the sounds of the gunshots may have echoed down the hill to anyone awake at 5 a.m. I'd managed to get the Walther into the holster without too much trouble. It was smaller than the 9mm Sig, but it looked neat enough. I left everything exposed—in case they wondered who had fired into the car and finished Junior. The blood on my shirt and inside the newly double-penetrated jacket didn't make me feel too happy. But, hey! I'm a survivor, okay?

Lana was faking a pretty good crying scene. Not overdoing it, just showing enough concern for the wounded man who saved her life. And that was where the story got… I'd say *interesting* but maybe *even weirder* would be better.

Of course, the police wanted the Walther, and my ID, and the story of my life—that is until Lana insisted that the local medical unit take me to the nearest hospital for attention. Thank God they let Lana ride with me. The problem was I really didn't know the story of my life, not as far as Lana and the Marcus family were concerned. A Tryon Police vehicle followed us to the hospital that wasn't far from a town called Columbus and the interstate. They obviously were not going to let me out of their sight till they got some sort of explanation for the gunfire, the smashed vehicles, and more excitement than the little towns around there had seen since the railroad stopped running.

Getting out of my shirt and jacket—now evidence, and getting the wound cleaned up for inspection gave me more pain than any part of Jerome's more deadly wounding. A fair-sized strip of skin had been torn, burned, and contaminated with bits of leather. I didn't see the X-rays, but the emergency room doc said there was a chip or crack in the seventh rib. My lungs were clear and some artery wasn't bleeding, but they wanted to keep me overnight and recheck things in the morning. Not a problem with me, but I needed to talk to Lana in private. I got lucky again—I got a private room. But by 10 a.m. it was almost a crowd scene.

Private or not, it didn't matter as far as the North Carolina State Police were concerned. Medically I wasn't critical, so they could interrogate me—and they tried. Lana was on the verge of screaming till they agreed to let her stay. Of course, with my pain, it was easier to let her answer the more involved questions. I was such a wimp.

No, we were not actually married as we had let Monica at the Medford Inn believe. We had been making plans, but… And, yes, we had met in Virginia where Lana was operating a bed-and-breakfast.

Even though she still had connections with the Marcus organization, she had left Nevada to get away from Allen Marcus Junior who was an abusive bully. The senior Marcus had been helping her and trying to get help for his son but to no avail. The father had come to Asheville and had finally located Junior but only found him less reasonable. One of the father's employees had discovered that Allen Junior was staying in a motel near the interstate outside of Columbus and called early that morning to warn us to leave. The timing might have been better. Then it was my turn, and they would wait for the answers.

"Why were you carrying a gun?" asked the detective.

"Marcus Junior accosted me outside of Jeffry Cobb's real estate office and warned me to stay away from Lana. I have a permit to carry, good in North and South Carolina, so why not? And, yes, I usually practice in commercial ranges once or more a month. I'm a writer, and I write bloody stuff."

"Who fired first?"

"I heard the car tearing out of the parking space then the tires skidding. I pulled the Walther and started to bring it up when I heard the first shot and felt the pain. I went to the two-handed grip and

saw the flash of his second shot as I started to fire."
I knew what the next question would be. I hoped
my memory for sound patterns was good. "Six times,
maybe seven. Three double-taps—yeah, one more.
Seven. Full clip."

"Do either of you know where the driver's second
shot went?"

"Two holes in my jacket," I said. "One in, one out.
And Lana's not wounded anywhere…" I shrugged.

Lana just sat with a beautifully concerned look.

"Might check the tree," I added.

"One other thing," the detective said. "The Walther is not registered to you. It seems to belong to
a collector out in Nevada who is deceased. It has a
German serial number going back to World War II.
The slide's engraved 7.65 mm, not .32 auto. It's a real
antique. Can you tell me how you got it?"

Thank God Lana took over.

"It's not his. It's mine," she said. "Well, Allen Senior
gave it to me before I left Nevada. He had two of
them. He said they were gifts from the old man who
was a friend of his."

"My Sig 9mm was hidden in my car," I said. "She
gave the Walther to me in the room, just in case."
That seemed to satisfy them.

It was almost one o'clock when the North Carolina officers and the county sheriff left.

I was offered a lunch, which really didn't appeal to me. Lana came and stood close. She put her arms around my neck and her mouth close to my ear.

"You good with the story? Everything clear?" she whispered.

I turned to answer her just as softly. "Just one thing," I said. "Who the hell wrote the script? I'm tired of getting shot."

CHAPTER 11

It was almost dark. Lana was asking around to see if there was a taxi service that could take her back to the Medford in Tryon. One of the hospital volunteers lived near there, but Lana would have to wait until the shift change. Then suddenly it was a non-issue. Allen Marcus Senior walked into the room. He looked relaxed and well-tailored— as usual. I wondered if I needed the Sig or maybe Lana's apron. Then he smiled. Somehow, it was not comforting.

"I'm afraid that my son and his friend Jerome have not been very kind to you."

"I was beginning to wonder if I had accidentally insulted you or your hotels in one of my books."

"Well," he laughed, "not that I know of. But it does seem that Junior found you in the way of an unfortunately ill-conceived project of his. I would apologize for him, but I'm not sure it would ease your pain." Marcus went to the other chair, turned it to face the bed instead of the television set, and made himself comfortable. "For what it may be worth to you, I've hired a very good lawyer in Asheville to watch over the process here. Since there was a violent death involved, it seems likely that the local judiciary will want to be involved in some way. If they want an appearance bond for you or whatever… Well, he'll take care of all of that." Marcus looked for a few seconds at Lana. He smiled briefly then he turned back to me. He had carried a small leather folder into the room, which I hadn't noticed until he held it up.

"All of the documents Jersey could find in your car…" He handed the pouch to Lana. "An automotive repair facility on the edge of town found that the impact had an unfortunate effect on the frame of your nice sporty vehicle. They believe they can convince the insurance company that it is…I think the word is *totaled*. When you're free to go and feeling better, decide what you want, and I'll be happy to take care of it. Jersey will stay in touch with you. He wanted me to tell you there is a trade he thinks the two of you should make. I assume you know what he has in mind."

I did. But getting the Walther back from the local law might take a while. Perhaps that was something for the Asheville lawyer to do.

A few crazy years back, I had cracked a rib in a skiing accident involving a tree. I remember it hurt for several weeks, even with a special chest-binder. I was pretty damn sure this wasn't going to leave me feeling any better. Try to lie back—it hurt. Try to turn over—it hurt. Sit up—it hurt. Cough—oh, hell! And, of course, the lovely nurses were trying to get me to breathe deeply and cough about every two hours.

Johnathan Fulton, Esq. had made it down to the hospital outside of Columbus a little after 9 a.m. following a very restless night. He listened to my complaints of pain, and during the morning medical rounds, was able to convince the doctors I should not be discharged. His argument almost had me convinced that since I would be required to live in a motel for some time while all the legal concerns were being addressed, and since this would not permit me to enjoy all the comforts of home, it certainly seemed more medically sound to not discharge me until the wound had healed and I could move as necessary without pain. Of course, driving to the hospital—if I had a car—would be a problem with the rib pain. And then my dear friend—but not wife—could be required at any time to return to her business in Virginia. The physicians agreed that therapy for keeping the lungs clear and follow-up X-rays would be necessary. So, for five to seven days, they would see how it went.

And then we repeated the answers to everything Lana and I had been asked by the state and county law enforcement personnel. It was fascinating to listen to him get some elements of our stories not quite as we told it then jump on the differences and begin to shift the blame for the shooting away from Junior. *Jeez…lawyers!* And the painful truth is, there were a few minutes when I wondered just who this guy was working for. Finally, I just stopped talking and looked at him. He knew why.

"I'm sure you both see what a few small discrepancies in your stories could do if the county or district attorney wanted to bring this to trial. I feel quite certain they will not, but… We must be prepared." He closed the thin leather notebook, stood, and moved closer to the bed. "I am, however, reasonably certain that they will want a recorded version of what you told the detectives and a printed copy of it that they will want you to sign as a sworn statement. If, *if*, you carefully recall and repeat that statement, I believe they will declare it an act of self-defense and dismiss the whole matter. Do you understand the importance of that testimony?"

Two days later, I rode a wheelchair into a somewhat ornate, heavily wooded conference room of the hospital. The detectives, three more attorneys, and a woman with a shorthand machine sat on one side of the table. Lawyer Fulton, Allen Marcus, and Lana sat on the other side, leaving a place for me in the middle. Lana smiled warmly and patted my hand. Nice touch.

The deposition or testimony or whatever it was went smoothly enough. Mr. Fulton only had to object twice, both times about who got shot with what gun and where. It seems that Marcus Junior had carried two guns, both Glocks, one a long barrel 9 mm, which he had in his hand and had fired. He also had a shorter barreled .380 caliber that contained some custom-made ammunition that was still being examined. When asked, the detectives confirmed that it was the 9 mm bullet that had struck me. Mr. Fulton shared his frustration about not having been told this before the hearing. The detectives and lawyers on that side of the table looked uncomfortable. I wondered how Fulton had found out.

There were a couple of other wrinkles that made me glad the hospital courtesy box provided a tube of antiperspirant. "Did you push Miss Lawrence down, or if she wasn't hit, why did she fall?"

"When I heard the car revving the engine and the tires screeching, I started to draw the pistol she had given me and shouldered her toward the tree. Then I heard and felt the first gunshot and…then the second shot from the car, and I'm not really sure what happened to her then, but I think she fell on the roots of that huge old tree. May have saved her life."

"You've admitted that…" the district attorney started to ask, and again, Mr. Fulton objected.

"He made a free statement to one of your detectives. I don't really believe you could call that an admission of anything, do you?"

"Very well then. You stated that the weapon you used in killing Mr.—"

"Objection again, sir. Shooting and defending himself, we'll agree to."

The attorney across the table took a deep breath. "You have stated that the pistol you used…that you fired, was not your usual weapon. The coroner has stated that four of the shots you fired were probably fatal—at least three she is sure of. If that wasn't your usual weapon, one you have practiced with, how do you explain your accuracy?"

Now I took a deep breath. "Well, sir… I do practice shooting on commercial ranges every month or so, and with different handguns. And the fact is, I do own a Walther PPK like the one Lana, Miss Lawrence, gave me. It's in my gun safe in Virginia." And then I caught myself just before my big mouth and bigger ego got me in real trouble. What I started to say was, "And fact is, sir, only four hits out of seven—even at night with only street lights—wouldn't be considered very accurate with most of the people I shoot with." Ouch… Too close, too close.

When the North Carolina people had finished with me, Fulton asked to include Allen Marcus's testimony. He stood, took the oath, and sat with a look of sadness on his face I had not seen before.

"Mr. Marcus, Miss Lana Lawrence told the county detectives that you gave her the Walther pistol that was used in this unfortunate affair. Is that correct?"

"It is, sir."

"And how did you happen to have the gun?"

"A very good and rather old friend, a collector of weapons, gave me two of them. He's now deceased."

"I am told that the one in evidence is in near mint condition, and as a World War II antique, it's worth quite a bit of money."

Allen Marcus gave a somewhat non-committal nod of the head.

"Will you tell us why you gave such a valuable weapon to a young woman with no previous experience with guns?"

Marcus looked down silently for a few minutes. "My son had tried to force a romantic affair upon Miss Lawrence, who refused. On the second refusal, he became violent and struck her repeatedly. An employee had seen his violence, and he struck the employee also. The police were called, and I learned that this was not his first attack on women. It was an expensive situation, but I kept my son out of prison. But his…attention to Miss Lawrence began all over again. It was then I gave her the pistol."

"Did she know how to use it?"

"No, but one of my associates had military training and took her out into the desert to give her some experience. I made certain my son knew about this. The idea was to scare him away, not to set her up to shoot him."

"And?"

"Didn't seem to work. He said some nasty things about any woman who tried to shoot him... Unless... Well, he was sure he'd get them first. I arranged for a guard around Lana most of the time. She learned about the possibility of casinos opening in Virginia and wanted to investigate it and get away from Las Vegas. I made that possible for her."

"Mr. Marcus, do you believe that your son, Allen Junior, was actually trying to shoot to kill this man you just listened to?"

"From things I'd heard him say over the last month or so, I believe he was primarily trying to kill Miss Lawrence, and if this gentleman was in the way, he was just... He said he would just be collateral damage. He actually used that term... Just collateral damage."

Then they heard Lana, who remembered little except the dash of the car, the gunfire, and falling over something. They hadn't asked her if she knew Marcus Junior. I thought letting Senior fill that in worked rather well. It also gave Lana a chance to look very sad and blot her eyes. Fine actress.

And, of course, Monica Dolan had testified about how she knew us. We were such a sweet couple—even if we weren't married…yet. The chambermaids hadn't mentioned seeing any guns in our room. We just seemed so nice. She thought we were looking for a place to live in the area and suggested we might ask Jeffry Cobb, a realtor she knew I had been seeing. One of the local detectives leaned over the shoulders of the state's attorneys and was obviously shaking this off as unnecessary. Actually, I'd like to have heard what he had to say about Junior stopping me in his parking lot. Could have been interesting. Something had scared Cobb back into his office. Probably the pistol Junior had carried on his hip.

The coroner's report and my medical record were accepted by both sides of the table.

And now it was obvious that all the necessary questions had been asked as far as the state of North Carolina was concerned. Lana, Allen Marcus, and I knew there was one missing element, and one we would not mention: Jersey.

CHAPTER 12

Unless you are really into all the legal ins and outs of cases like this, you would probably find the ending of this one an anticlimactic bore. I got to stay in the hospital most of another week while they figured out a way to make self-defense look good to everybody as a reason for not bringing me to trial. And the longer I stayed in that room, even with Lana for company most of the day, the antsier I got. Night after night, I saw Jersey leaning over with the Walther and wanting my Sig. And I asked myself, "Why the hell was I so easy?" I could have tried to tell myself the pain made me do it. But I know I couldn't make myself believe it.

And so…after almost two years, I've decided the answer was fucking obvious, and I'll just have to live with it.

It was all in my crotch. I'm a guy! I want to do things and fix things. And worse than that, I'm a guy who writes action stuff with broads and blood. And there I was, shot, next to a beautiful broad, who I was afraid had been shot too, and worse, a lovely piece I hadn't protected. And then, something like a deus ex machina in a dark grey tailored suit steps in to make me the hero. Crap!

If I'd had any idea of all the mess, how close I'd come to going on trial for having the gun that just killed a man but a gun I'd never fired… I'd told so many damn lies I really needed Tina around with her steno pad to help me keep track of them. And… I know there is no statute of limitation on murder, but I don't know about killing in self-defense and perjury for Christ's sake… With all that in mind, I'm probably living with Scotch and sleeping pills for a while, and I obviously can't publish this thing in my own name.

Lana had collected all my gear from the Medford Inn—everything but the bullet-ripped new leather jacket and polo shirt—packed it neatly and brought it to my hospital room. Yeah, it still hurt to move some, especially my ribs on the right. They gave me a chest-girdle that fastened with Velcro. I could manage.

The nurse insisted that I ride in a wheelchair to the driveway and Allen Marcus's waiting Lincoln. The leather suit bag lay in my lap and the backpack hooked to the chair. Lana reached down and took my hand as the nurse pushed. I thought that was nice.

Jersey drove, and Allen Marcus sat in front for a change. Lana and I had the back seat to ourselves. There was a small attaché-like case between us. It held my Sig Sauer.

"The attorney, Mr. Fulton, convinced the county sheriff's office to give back the Walther," Allen Marcus said. "The state wanted to keep it for their museum—or so they said. At any rate, it is back and so is your weapon. Things may actually be getting back to normal."

I swallowed the explosion. Normal? This was normal? A painful healing rib and damn near indicted for shooting a man with a gun I'd never fired! Oh, please… I took a deep breath, and another, and let it go.

We did the double traffic circles outside of Columbus and made the turn down onto I-26 and headed north. It took me a while to get comfortable. Finally, I had to ask.

"We headed for Asheville?"

"Just the airport. A small group of us from Las Vegas are meeting with some senators and congressmen this week."

"Works for me," I said. "Home's only a few miles out of town."

"I'm afraid that's not in the cards, my friend," Marcus said. "A press conference is already scheduled, and you'll be a bit of a distraction. There seems to be too much gunfire around you. Sorry."

Was I hearing this right? All the gunfire had come from the Allen Marcus side of the fence. The only thing I had done was lose some blood. I guess Lana saw the pink flush starting in my neck. She squeezed my hand hard and looked at me with a raised eyebrow. I got the message. Painful to accept, but there it was.

Jersey handed his boss a rather thick brown envelope. Marcus took a quick look and handed it to me.

"This Lincoln's a rental," Marcus said. "You're welcome to use it a couple of months or as long as you need to. The papers are all there. Right, Jersey?"

"Papers and debit card. Yes, sir."

"And settle up with your insurance company for your car. When you find what you want, there are some papers and a Nevada number to call. Take your time. Get what you like. Well…maybe not a Rolls or Ferrari, but…nice enough." He laughed.

There wasn't much else to say for the rest of the thirty-minute trip. Bits of a lot of things kept popping into my head, but silence seemed better. The piece I couldn't ignore had hit me the night after the recorded hearing. This guy, Marcus, would have been a fit for the Corleone family. Sure, Junior was bad enough, and a family traitor besides, but Allen Senior had to have been as cool as Al Pacino in *The Godfather* to set up a hit on his own son. That bit of emotion at the hearing? Suddenly it didn't impress me. What now seemed very important was to take the crumbs this guy was offering me and get the hell out of his life.

And Jersey? About him—I still didn't know. What I did know was that it was no longer important to get close enough to find out.

We parked on the private ramp at the airport, only a few steps from the airstair of the Gulfstream jet with *MARCUS HOTELS AND CASINOS* painted on the side. One of the plane's uniformed crewmen opened the car door for Allen Marcus. He gave me a brief wave then headed toward the plane. Lana leaned toward me and gave me a peck, and Jersey helped her out of the car. I walked around and leaned on the driver's door. Everyone had been inside the plane, but suddenly the stairway started back down. Lana came out of the cabin waving something at me. I walked toward the plane to meet her.

"I forgot to give you back your credit card," she said. "I didn't really hurt it much. Don't worry." She took another step toward me and slipped her arms around my neck.

"We'll always have Asheville," she said with a smile. After a warm kiss on the lips, she was gone, leaving me the card and that great Dior scent. The breeze on the ramp helped me enjoy the sight of those wonderful legs as she climbed the stairs back into the jet.

I called Jeffry Cobb. He'd put everything on hold until he was sure I was either out of hospital or jail. I told him I was free of iron bars and nurses. He laughed. Then I told him to go ahead and nail down the bluff property if he could. He was sure we had it. I told him I had to make a trip to Germany and to leave a message with Tina if there was a problem.

I had no idea what getting the dog back into the US would involve, but I was pretty sure the Germans did. It was their business. And then Tina gave me one more jolt.

My last published novel had been bought by a major studio. Part of the deal was I had to work on the screenplay. I love the Hollywood money, but the people… Anyway, if I was there, I might be able to keep the story together. It's about two lawyers, a guy in San Francisco, and a woman in LA. The fact is they're lawyers, yes, but they both are brokers for *hit men*—at least in San Francisco—and *hit women* in Los Angeles. They decide they don't want the competition, and that's where the fun begins.

For sex and violence, it's a pretty good story—if you're into that sort of thing.

The End

ABOUT THE AUTHOR

Paul Buchanan is a retired physician, flight surgeon, commercial pilot, and flight instructor. He is a former NASA executive and was crew physician for at least two historic NASA missions. He is the author or coauthor of dozens of articles published in medical and scientific journals, many having to do with the physiological and life-support issues to be faced in future long-duration space missions. On retirement from NASA, Paul turned his attention to writing fiction, this book being just the third of many installments. Read and enjoy with the comfort of knowing there is much more just waiting for you!